25 Years of Magical Reading

ALADDIN PAPERBACKS
EST. 1972

First Aladdin Paperbacks edition October 1997
Copyright © 1993 by Joan Walsh Anglund
Aladdin Paperbacks
An imprint of Simon & Schuster Children's Publishing Division
1230 Avenue of the Americas, New York, NY 10020
Also available in a Simon & Schuster Books for Young Readers edition.
The text of this book was set in 15 point Weiss.
The illustrations were done in pen, ink, and watercolor.
Printed and bound in the United States of America
10   9   8   7   6   5   4   3   2   1
The Library of Congress has cataloged the hardcover edition as follows:
Anglund, Joan Walsh. [Bedtime book]
A bedtime book / by Joan Walsh Anglund.
p.   cm.
Summary: Story-poems about apples, dragons, princesses, trees, rainbows, and friends.
1. Children's stories. American. [1. Stories in rhyme. 2. Short stories.] I. Title.
PZ8.3.A549Be   1992
[E]—dc20
91-29529   CIP
ISBN 0-671-74176-4
ISBN 0-689-81702-9 (Aladdin pbk.)

JOAN WALSH ANGLUND

A BEDTIME BOOK

ALADDIN PAPERBACKS

For Emily and Thaddeus' summer friends

Jamie	Megan	Cara	Sammy	Mary
Chris	Caitlin	Christina	Teddy	Will
Maggie	Sean	Jacy	Bram	Ward
Kate	Merrill	Aaron	Tara	David
Lucy	Annie	Graham	Nyle	Shep
Hannah	Jake	Alex	Jonathan	Eddie

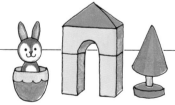

A TABLE OF CONTENTS

MY FRIEND
THE TREE

I have a friend.
He is very tall.

He doesn't say much,
    but he's always there for me,
and I always know
    just where to find him.

My friend is big and green.
    He likes to hold me in his arms
        whenever I need a cozy rest
            all by myself.

Sometimes
    we just like to sit quietly,
        side by side,
            and listen
                to the wind's song
                    together.

My friend helps me
in special ways.

When it's hot,
his shade keeps me cool.

When it's rainy,
he keeps me dry.

Sometimes,
at night,
he whispers leafy lullabies
to help me fall asleep.

And, when I need
a place to swing,
he doesn't mind at all.

In the spring,
  he invites all the birds
    to stay with us
      awhile.

In the summer,
  he holds up my house
    and makes a roof of green
      to shelter me.

In the fall,
　　he showers me
　　　　with golden stars.

In the winter,
　　he tickles the sky
　　　　with his long fingers
　　till all
　　　　the snow spills down.

My friend is lovable.
  Toadstools and bunnies
    like to snuggle next to him.

Squirrels use him for a highway.

Hummingbirds and butterflies
  recommend him to their friends.

My friend is tall and strong
  and very special.

I like my friend, the tree.

THE STORY OF ME, TOO

Merrell took a stick, stuck it in the sand, and said,
   "Look. I can write my own name."

And little Annie said, "Me, too."

(But somehow Annie's letters got all mixed-up
   when *she* tried it.)

Merrell said, "See, I can draw a birthday cake, too."

And little Annie said, "Me, too."
   (But somehow, when Annie tried it,
   the candles all drooped a little.)

Merrell got out her new paint box
and said, "I can
paint a rainbow."

And little Annie said,
"Me, too."

(But somehow all *her* colors melted together
and turned into a little brown puddle on the floor.)

Merrell said, "My doll is getting married today
and I can put on her wedding dress and veil
all by myself."

And little Annie said, "Me, too."

(But somehow, *her* doll's shoes didn't fit,
and the buttons wouldn't button, and
the veil got all tangled and
the dress went on backwards.)

Merrell said, "I can help fix dinner.
   I can stir the pudding."

And little Annie said, "Me, too."

(But somehow, when Annie stirred the pudding,
   it missed the bowl, and jumped right on
      her new pink dress instead.)

Merrell said, "I can climb a tree."
   And little Annie said, "Me, too."

(But somehow the branches
   were too high and
   Annie's legs were too
   short, and the twigs
   scratched her and her
   mother had to come
   out and get her
   down again.)

Merrell said, "Let's play 'dress-up.'
    I can be grown up just like Mommy."

And little Annie said, "Me, too."
(But somehow, she couldn't walk in the high heels,
and she tripped over the long skirts and scarves,
and she couldn't see because the big floppy
hat got in the way.)

Merrell said, "I can fly a kite."

And little Annie said, "Me, too."
(But somehow Annie's kite wouldn't go up,
        and when it did, she couldn't get it down,
            and then the string broke,
                and the kite blew away
                and disappeared over the trees.)

Merrell said, "I'm almost five years old,
and I don't have to go to bed early."

And little Annie said, "Me, too."

(But somehow her little golden head
nodded, and her little blue eyes
began to droop, then the dreams
began to come, and soon
little Annie was fast asleep.)

Good night, little "Me, too."
Tomorrow is another day ...for trying.

THE LITTLE BOY AND THE PRINCESS

One morning,
a little boy went walking.

He walked
and he walked all around
until suddenly he knew he was lost!

Then he sat down on a rock,
and cried.

But a princess came along

and she took him to her castle

and gave him a ride
   on her merry-go-round.

Then they had ice cream cones
   for lunch

and the little boy didn't feel
   like crying anymore.

They played games together
and colored with crayons
all afternoon.

Then she drove him home
to his mother.

Moral:
If you ever get lost,
it's best to get found
by a princess!

A SILLY APPLE STORY

A silly apple was sitting in a tree.
It was bored,
    so it fell down.
It hit a little boy on the head
    and bounced right into his lap.
The little boy looked up
    and said, "Thank you, apple tree!"
and took that silly apple right home
    to make apple sauce for dinner.
Yum!

Moral:
If you're an apple sitting in a tree,
    don't get silly and fall down,
        or pretty soon you'll be
            somebody's apple sauce!

MY DRAGON

I have a little dragon
    who is very fond of me.
He lives down in the marshes,
    which are very near the sea.

    He frolics in the waves till dawn.
      I meet him on the shore.
    We gather conchs and scallops.
      We build castles by the score.

        And sometimes in our garden,
          beneath a shady tree,
        he spreads a linen tablecloth
          and serves us cakes and tea.

On rainy days we play at home
when no one is about
and, while my nanny's napping,
we dance and sing and shout.

We have the best adventures
...for dragons love to fly,
and when the weather's sunny
we soar across the sky.

We've visited Zimbabwe
and Australia and Siam.
We've perched on palace rooftops
while we shared some bread and jam.

We are always home by bedtime.
Long before the dark and gloom,
my friend has flown me safely
to my cozy upstairs room.

We whisk into my window
    and whisper our goodbyes:
"We'll meet again tomorrow!"
    Then away my dragon flies.

And as the evening darkens
    and the stars begin to shine,
I pray a special thank-you
    for that special friend of mine.

TO BE A BALLERINA

Each Wednesday, rain or shine,
    Jane packed her pink tote bag.
She put in her leotard, her tights, her ballet slippers
    and a soft white towel.

Each Wednesday, rain or shine,
    Jane climbed the stairs to the rehearsal hall,
      and joined the other young girls
        in the dressing room.

She put on her leotard, her tights and her ballet slippers
    and went in with the others to join the dance class.

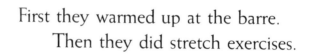

    First they warmed up at the barre.
      Then they did stretch exercises.

    They practiced the 5 arm positions.
      They practiced the 5 foot positions.

They remembered to keep their bodies straight,
their arms bent gracefully and
their toes pointed out.

For weeks they listened to the same music
as they practiced and practiced
their dance steps.

Their teacher, Miss Solomonoff,
was sometimes very strict.
Ballet was serious business, said Miss Solomonoff.
The dance class was not a place to play.
It was a place to work!

And...
if you worked hard enough,
and practiced long enough,
one day...
you might become a real ballerina!

Jane had seen a real ballerina,
   up on the big stage in the city,
when her grandfather had taken her to see
   her first real ballet...The Nutcracker.

Jane never forgot how beautiful
   it had been.
Ever since that day, Jane had wanted,
   with all her heart,
to be a real ballerina.

And so, Jane practiced,
   and little by little,
she got better and better.
And now, finally,
   it was time for their ballet
to be presented at the
dance recital.

The ballet that Jane was in was named
          "The Flower Garden." Each little
girl was to be a different flower, and
          Jane was to be a pink rose.

Her mother sewed her a beautiful costume
          of pink satin, and Jane wore
a crown of pink roses in her hair.

The day of the recital was so exciting,
          with all the musicians tuning up,
and everyone hurrying around backstage.

But soon, the lights dimmed, the audience
          hushed, and the music started.
The ballet recital was beginning.

Jane stood backstage, listening to the
          music as the first dance began.
The older girls did their dance first,
          then the littler girls did a
clown number. The audience
          laughed and clapped
as they tumbled about.

Then, Jane knew it was her turn.
Her heart pounded as she heard the
familiar music begin to play.

Then, suddenly,
    she was leaping in the air, and
she was spinning and dancing to
    the music, and her heart was
so happy she wanted the dance
    never to end.

She felt lighter and happier than she'd ever felt before.
The music was all about her and it seemed to lift her up
    and carry her along on beautiful waves of sound…
        twirling…swirling…around and around.

Then, all at once, it was over
    …and it was time to bow
        and curtsy,
    and everyone was clapping
        and cheering…

...and then, the curtain came down
and her arms were filled with
a big bouquet of roses.

Now Jane realized that, finally,
after all the Wednesdays of practice,
and all the weeks of hard work,
she was a
Real
Ballerina
at last!

A RAINBOW STORY

Once, after a great storm,
  a little rainbow was born,
    and it grew and grew,
      and arched itself across the sky.

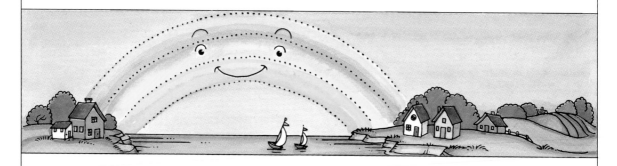

It was bright and lovely
  and sparkled with many colors.

It was a happy little rainbow, as it
  stretched out its arms from side to side.
It smiled and sparkled while it waited,
  way up high, for someone to notice it.

But no one came to see it.

All the people just stayed inside their houses,
    with their doors and windows closed.

So, after a little while,
    the little rainbow got discouraged,
and sadly folded away all its bright colors,
    and faded back up into the sky
        where no one could ever find it.
        Poor little rainbow.

        Poor silly people!

HUG AND KISS

A Tale of Two Kittens

Once there were two kittens.
One was named Hug.
The other was named Kiss.
They were sisters.

All day long, in the sunshine, they played together.
All night long, in the moonlight, they played together
    (with little catnaps in between to keep up their energy).

Together, they played many games.
They played Pounce or Climb the Pole
    or Catch the Yarn or Follow the Butterfly.

But sometimes, instead of playing together,
    they did mean things to each other,
        as sisters sometimes do.

Kiss would bite Hug's tail,
    and Hug would scratch Kiss's ear.

One day, they were so busy being naughty,
    they forgot to be careful.

Their mother had always told them
    to stay away from the deep water,
but they forgot to mind her,
    got too close to the edge, and oh!
      splash!...they fell in.

Poor Hug and Kiss!
    They almost drowned.

But just in time,
      their mother caught them, and
            she never let go until they were both
                  safe and sound on dry land.

After that, Hug and Kiss
      decided to be good little sisters,
            and they didn't fight anymore.

They only played
      together sweetly
            (most of the time),

which made their
      mother very
      happy.

CAROLINE

One day after school, a little girl came home.
　　Her mother was not there.
Her father was not there.
　　But a gentle cow was there,
　　　so the little girl felt better.
The girl's name was Emily.

The cow didn't have a name,
　　so Emily named her Caroline.

Emily and Caroline
    took a walk through the meadow.
Emily picked clover,
    and Caroline ate it.
Emily picked daisies,
    and Caroline ate them as well,
        but she liked the clover better.

Emily and Caroline
    sat beside a stream, and
Emily told Caroline a long sleepy story.
    But Caroline wouldn't take a nap,
        so after a while Emily chased butterflies
            while Caroline just chewed.

It was a pleasant afternoon, filled with
    butterflies and bees, meadow grass and sunshine,
        but soon it was time to go home.

Emily waved goodbye to Caroline at the gate,
    and Caroline walked slowly
        down the road, still chewing.

That night,
    Emily dreamt of a gentle cow
       who came to her window to give her
        a ride on her broad back.

They soared past the treetops,
    and over the church steeple,
       and up through the clouds,
        and higher…to the stars.

Then, together,
    they jumped right over the moon!

How they giggled
as down they
both tumbled,
over and over
through the
deep blue sky…

…till they fell, happy and tired
into a huge, soft haystack,
where they snuggled together
and dreamed.

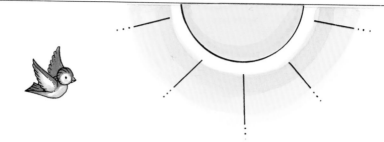

When Emily woke up, the sun was shining,
    and all the birds were awake and singing.
Emily was there,
    and her mother was there,
        and her father was there,
but when she went to look,
    Caroline was nowhere to be found.

But down at the gate, cool and sweet,
    was a jug of creamy fresh milk,
        just right for Emily's breakfast.

"Thank you, Caroline," whispered Emily,
    and went to begin her new day.